PORTAL MAGIC

A RHAPTAVERSE NOVELLA

LILY SKYY

Portal Magic
Copyright © 2022 by Lily Skyy
www.LilySkyy.com

First Edition: June 2022

ISBN 978-1-957989-39-6 (ebook)
ISBN 978-1-960207-32-6 (print)

Published by Books to Hook Publishing, LLC.
www.BooksToHook.com

CONTENTS

PART ONE
CHOOSING DAY

CHOOSING DAY

Ashar bolted through the alley and out onto the boulevard beyond, startling a man carrying a basket of mangoes. He ignored the indignant shouting as he flew down the white limestone road, dodging pedestrians going about their early morning routine.

It was not his fault he was late; the fried plantains in the market had smelled especially delicious this morning so of course he had to make a stop on his way to school. The seller had also decided to make a bowl of the plantains ten shillings —nine more than he had—so it had taken him a few extra minutes to lose the guards in the chaos of the market.

Ashar licked the remnants of his breakfast from his fingers as he narrowly avoided an oncoming cart. His nimble feet were well-versed in this mad dash though, and Ashar only smiled as the cart driver yelled at him to get out of the way. When the school came into view, he slowed to a jog and made his way up the path to the front doors. The school was situated just south of the central plaza in the great city of Rhapta. Most of the city, including the school, was made of white limestone that helped reflect the incessant heat of the African sun. Even this early in the morning, sweat beaded on the back of Ashar's neck. As he stepped inside the door, the shade was a welcome respite.

He hurried down the silent hall toward his classroom and thankfully the door had been left open. The teacher was just telling the class to quiet down so they could get started and Ashar breathed a sigh of relief. His uncle would have been furious with him if he got into trouble again for being late, which was most days. Ashar had been told on many occasions that his schooling was the most important thing in his life, especially due to his...predicament. He took his seat at the back of the room by the door.

Good morning, class, came the voice of Teacher Fardia into the minds of all the students.

Good morning, Teacher, replied the class in unison back to her. The ability to speak telepathically was a universal ability for the citizens of Rhapta; something that the rest of the world did not share. Inside the city walls, speaking out loud was generally frowned upon but had started becoming slightly more accepted since the crowning of the new queen a year ago.

Teacher Fardia had a bright smile as she looked over her students this morning. *Today is a very exciting day, class. Who remembers what today is?*

A girl in a bright yellow dress raised her hand. *Today is the day we pick out apprenticeships!*

Very close, Teacher Fardia said, lacing her hands together. *Students don't pick their official apprenticeships until age seventeen. Today, though, you get to pick an apprenticeship that you would like to shadow for the next four years.* Pacing across the front of the room, she continued as many students shifted in their seats with eagerness. *Do not be mistaken, even though this is not your official choosing, this is still a very important decision of your life. Shadowing a mentor can give you real insights into what that career would be like. Most students end up making the apprenticeship that they shadowed as their first choice when it comes time to apply when they are seventeen. Now, who can tell me a few of the important considerations one must keep in mind while choosing their apprenticeship?*

Several of the students raised their hands, and Ashar slouched lower in his chair, hoping he would not be noticed. It's not that he didn't like speaking, he just didn't like drawing attention to himself for a few key reasons.

Teacher Fardia called on a smaller boy aggressively waving his hand on the other side of the room. *Yes, Hamza, Please tell us,* she said with more patience than Ashar imagined possible.

Hamza sat up straight and spoke as if reciting from a text. *Apprenticeships in Rhapta are largely based on a person's abilities as they will shape our lives for the future. Apprenticeships almost always lead to the apprentice taking over the position of their mentor when it is time for the mentor to step down. There are many apprenticeships to choose from, regardless of one's ability.*

Two boys a few rows over from Ashar snickered and turned to him. *Assuming you* have *an ability,* the taller of the two whispered, barely containing his laughter.

Ashar found twenty-five pairs of eyes on him then. Suddenly, he felt a drop of water splash onto his face. Looking up, he found a tiny rain cloud forming above his head, sending droplets falling down onto his face. The laughter from the boys spread throughout the class.

That's enough, boys! Teacher Fardia said, her bright demeanor becoming cross as quickly as the rain had come. *Jibreel, you know you are not allowed to use your abilities in class!* she scolded the smaller boy that had laughed at Ashar.

Jibreel waved his fingers toward the clouds dripping water onto an aggravated Ashar and it slowly dispersed into nothingness. Teacher Fardia cast a withering eye at the boy long enough for him to wilt in his chair meekly before she continued her lesson.

Now, she said, moving on, *Hamza was correct. Your apprenticeship and your subsequent profession are chosen with your abilities in mind, but there are many professions that are perfectly suited to those without any abilities.*

Ashar could have sworn she gave him a pitying look. He had been receiving those looks for over two years now and he had come to the conclusion that he would be getting them for the rest of his life.

Everyone received their ability in their tenth year, but if you hadn't received it by your eleventh then it was very rare that you would have one at all. It was not unheard of to not have an ability, but generally those who never gained any lived very poor lives. Most of those without abilities used to end up living in the outskirts just outside the city walls. That was up until the new queen came in and made the abandoned southern quarter of the city available for use for those on the outskirts who wanted a better life.

Ashar was already accustomed to the life, though. He and his uncle had been two of the hundreds of people who had moved from the outskirts to the southern quarter last year, taking up residence in one of the abandoned homes that had sat in ruin for decades.

Up until then, he and his uncle had lived in little more than a shack outside the city walls, his uncle picking up odd jobs where he could. Uncle Adil had no abilities just like Ashar, but now that they lived inside the city, it was easier for him to find work. Still, they had little money and Ashar didn't have the heart to ask his uncle for any. So Ashar had gotten good at slipping in and out of the city markets, taking food when he really needed it. He had gotten even better at not getting caught, too. On several occasions, he had pointed out to an angry guard or two that it was embarrassing that a grown man could not catch a thirteen-year-old boy, and one without abilities at that.

Teacher Fardia continued talking about the apprenticeships while Ashar looked around the room and wished he were anywhere else. Every single one of the other students in this class, and the rest of the school, had an ability. There were even a couple of children who had two, and that was rare.

Whenever Ashar was out in the city, running through the streets, climbing the baobab trees, or climbing onto abandoned rooftops, he never was self-conscious for a second over his lack of ability. But the moment he stepped into his school, it hit him in the face that every single one of them had a bright future after they graduated, and Ashar would still be stealing scraps.

Ashar stared out of the window at the sunny street as Teacher Fardia listed off the list of approved mentors and their respective professions the students could choose from. The apprenticeships with the warriors in the city seemed to be the most popular, followed by a few options within the scholars and healers.

Some of the students whispered excitedly over the apprenticeship with one of the queen's attendants. The queen herself was always a prominent topic of conversation in the city during this first year of her reign, seeing as she came to the throne in one of the darkest times in Rhaptan history. Many called this the beginning of a golden era but Ashar didn't see how the city could be considered prosperous when there were so many people who lived in poverty every day.

As Teacher Fardia made her way down the list toward the less desirable apprenticeships, one of them caused a bit of laughter to ripple throughout the class. *And then we have Ifran Toma who is a shopkeeper in the eastern district.*

Students tried to hide their giggling at that. Everyone knew

Ifran, he was the owner of a small antiques shop, but it would be better to call it a junk shop. The scatterbrained old man collected items he thought were worth a fortune by the dozen, shoving them onto overflowing shelves in hopes customers would see their worth.

Ashar had gone inside a few times to check it out. It would be the easiest thing to grab a few items and sneak right back out under Ifran's snoring nose, but even Ashar could not find anything worthwhile in there. Being Ifran's apprentice would be the most boring job in the entire city.

Mshai, the taller boy who had laughed at him, and Jibreel were sneaking glances toward Ashar and laughing again. The rain that had fallen on his shirt earlier had not even dried but he knew what was coming so he slunk down in anticipation.

Ashar, Mshai said, innocently. *I think you would be great at that apprenticeship. It would work great with your ability to be late every day since Ifran is practically senile. He'd forget he had an apprentice every morning!* Mshai and the rest of the class had dissolved into hysterical laughter before he made it to the end of his sentence. Ashar's ears were burning.

And what apprenticeship do you think you're going to get, Mshai? Warrior? With an ability to jump like a rabbit? The scathing voice came from two seats ahead of Asher.

Mshai's smile melted off his face like butter in a hot pan. *Of course I am!* he said defensively. *Nasrin, you know the warriors need applicants with physical abilities!*

I don't think they are looking for a glorified rabbit, Nasrin said. Laughter erupted among the students again and even Mshai's friend Jibreel was having a hard time concealing his laughter.

Ashar leaned to the side of his seat to look a few desks up at Nasrin who had turned to him with a small smile and a shrug as if to say, *I tried.*

While Ashar had stopped trying to defend himself, Nasrin

found it to be her civic duty to verbally pulverize those who tried to pick on him. She said they would not stop unless he stood up for himself but Ashar knew people responded to him very differently from the way they responded to her.

Like Ashar, Nasrin had come from the outskirts to the southern quarter last year, but that's where their similarities ended. Since they were little, Ashar knew Nasrin would excel at anything she did in life. She was the only child of two parents without abilities, yet she had acquired hers at the prodigious age of nine.

That was on top of the fact that she had always been an exceptional student and well-liked by everyone. Not to mention, she was beautiful as well. Her amber-brown eyes gave Mshai and Jibreel one more narrowed glare before facing forward at Teacher Farida's behest.

Ashar tuned out the teacher's voice for the remainder of the class until they were released for a short break. *Don't forget that you are all picking your apprenticeships during our last class today!* Teacher Fardia called as the students packed away their things. Ashar quickly slipped out of his seat and was down the hall before most of the students had even gotten up.

As soon as he stepped outside, the tension released from his shoulders. There was a small courtyard on this side of the building with columns running around the edge and a fountain in the middle. Before any of the teachers came out, Ashar quickly climbed one of the columns, using the thick vines that wrapped around it as a handhold until he was able to climb onto the roof of the school.

He settled in and watched as children of varying ages poured out into the courtyard for their mid-morning break. Even though they were still on school grounds, many of the students disregarded the "no abilities" rule when they were outside.

From his vantage point, Ashar watched one boy send a small breeze toward a girl, ruffling the hem of her skirt. The girl turned to yell at him and at the same time, several mice came scurrying out from the shadows and cracks of the building to nibble at the boy's feet. The girl laughed as the boy shrieked.

Others displayed their abilities as some sort of prestige. An older girl Ashar had seen before had twin balls of violet flames in her hands. She boasted how she had a similar ability to the queen and several onlookers marveled at her in awe. Some abilities were more subtle; Ashar could see a boy with dreadlocks shift his skin to that of a snake and a gaggle of nearby girls yelped at the sight of him.

On the other side of the courtyard, a group of students sat down to study. One moment they were in the bright gaze of the sun, and the next, a boy waved a hand and a shadow that shouldn't physically exist enveloped the group in cool shade.

Ashar glanced down and saw the top of Nasrin's head, swiveling around as if looking for someone. The hundreds of tiny braids on her head were pulled back into a ponytail today and whipped back and forth with her movement. Ashar knew he should go talk to her, but before he did, two unsavory people walked up to Nasrin with hands behind their backs.

Hi, Nasrin, Mshai said to her with a half-smile. The obnoxious attitude from earlier was replaced with a bashfulness that made Ashar want to vomit.

Hey, Nas, Jibreel said, dancing on his feet.

Hello, you two, Nasrin replied. *Are you going to make fun of me too?* she asked.

No! Of course not, Mshai said. *We would never do that to you.*

You're super cool! Jibreel said. *We actually, uh...* Nasrin raised an eyebrow.

We actually wanted to give you something. We know it's your birthday, Mshai said, finally. *Here!* They both pulled out small bouquets of wildflowers and presented them to the girl. Ashar tried not to laugh.

Oh! Nasrin said, taking the small bouquets. *Thank you...I... uh, love these,* she said with a polite smile. The two boys looked like it was *their* birthday when Nasrin smiled yet it only made Ashar roll his eyes. Nasrin's gift was growth, especially plants and flowers, so the two birdbrains had thought she would like the flowers they ripped up from a field. Only Ashar knew that she secretly hated being given plants as a gift because she could just make them herself. She said it was a waste to pluck them anyways.

I'm glad you like them, Mshai said, nudging Jibreel.

Yeah, and we were wondering if you maybe wanted to hang out after school? Jibreel asked nervously.

Nasrin's smile turned awkward. *How kind of you,* she said. *I actually have to help my mom with something after school. But maybe another time!*

Ashar snorted a laugh and quickly rolled away from the edge of the building to avoid being seen. His laugh had been loud enough to cause the three on the ground to look up, but they would not see anything.

Okay! Mshai said, not catching on to Nasrin's rejection. *Well, let us know whenever works for you.* Nasrin smiled and nodded as the two boys waved at her and walked away, nudging each other and laughing the whole way.

Ashar lay on his back as soon as they left Nasrin. A voice floated up from the ground a moment later. *Ashar, get down here!* Nasrin called.

Ashar rolled onto his stomach to peek over the edge. He found an angry Nasrin looking up at him with hands on her hips. He could not entirely deny Mshai and Jibreel's awkwardness around her though. Today she had on a dark blue dress that crossed over one shoulder and left the other bare. Her dark skin glowed in the sun as her amber-brown eyes glared at him to hurry up and get down.

Ashar sighed and made his way over to the column and down the vines to the floor of the courtyard. Nasrin's face had shifted to one of concern as she walked over to him. *Are you okay?* she asked. *They were disgustingly rude to you today.*

I'm just fine, Ashar said, leaning against the column and tucking his hands in his pockets so as not to fidget. *I don't care what they say. Either way, it's not like I'll have much of a choice for an apprenticeship. I'll have to go with whoever gets stuck with me.*

There are plenty of good options! Nasrin said, throwing a hand up. *There's...* she touched her forehead as she thought. *There's the quarries!* she said.

I'd be stuck in the mines day and night, Ashar said.

Well, what about working for the agriculture sector? she suggested.

You'd be far better at that than me, Ashar said. *Besides, I'd be stuck under the sun, tending to the fields all day.*

There's always a need for scholars! Nasrin supplied. *It's become a very prestigious job since the queen has been working so closely with them.*

The side of Ashar's face scrunched up. *And be stuck in the library all day?*

Nasrin heaved a breath. *Ash, you have to do something. You can't just run around the streets all day, stealing food and annoying the guards. And yes, I know very well where you were this morning. You have cinnamon all over your face.*

No, I don't, Ashar grumbled, rubbing at his face. *And nobody wants someone without abilities. Either way, I don't want to be tied to some stupid job like that. Once you have an ability, the govern-ment just wants to use you up. It's not like I'd really get a choice in my profession if I did have an ability. Remember what Teacher*

Farida said? Our professions are dictated based on our abilities. So, you know what? I like not having an ability.

Nasrin just gave him a droll look. *Fine, then your studies should at least be a priority so you can have options.* Right then a bell rang by the door, signaling the end of their break. Nasrin and Ashar started walking with everyone else toward the door. She nudged his shoulder. *You didn't say happy birthday to me, by the way.*

Ashar ducked his head. *I didn't have money to get you anything,* he said quietly.

You know I don't want anything, Nasrin said, flicking her hair over her shoulder. *But if you want to give me a gift, then don't skip your classes anymore.*

Ashar knew she was right and that he should pay attention to his classes more. But the prospect of being stuck doing the same job over and over for the rest of his life made the day bleak and unexciting. He would just be another cog in the wheel; a useless cog since he had no abilities. The two of them went inside and separated to go to their next classes, and Ashar kept his word and didn't skip this one at least.

EVEN THOUGH ASHAR had a dislike for school, there was one class he actually enjoyed—excelled at even.

Human Studies.

As he entered the class, he sat by the window as Teacher Dev was organizing his materials up front. The mood in the class was very polarized. Students either loved or hated the class with vigor, but Ashar thought that Teacher Dev's enthusiastic personality would more than make up for it.

Good afternoon, class, Teacher Dev said, making a note in one of his books.

Good morning, Teacher Dev, the class replied as they were supposed to.

Today we are talking about the history of the Pacific Islands and their cultures, so take your seats and quiet down, Teacher Dev said. He had graying hair, but his eyes were alight when he looked over the class. *Did everyone complete the reading I assigned last week?*

There were various nodding heads and a few students who looked anywhere but at the teacher. Ashar had skimmed through the book, reading the parts he thought would be interesting.

Wonderful! Teacher Dev said. *Everyone take out your homework first and we will—*

Teacher Dev? one girl said, raising her hand. It was the same girl in the yellow dress from Ashar's first class. *When are we going to talk about how to travel and live in human cities? I want to be prepared for when we take down the barrier.*

Many students nodded their heads vigorously at this and all eyes were up front.

Teacher Dev laughed. *Oh, that is still a long way off. You don't need to worry about interacting with humans for a long time, young ones.*

But the queen said we would be able to leave the city and travel the world soon. What if we aren't prepared? a boy asked.

The room had gotten quiet and all of Ashar's attention was on Teacher Dev and what he would say. It was true that they could not travel the world nor enter human society; they could only study it. The great city of Rhapta had existed in the forests surrounding Mount Kilimanjaro for thousands of years, but soon after its creation, the king had wrapped the city in an invisible psychic barrier, cutting it off from the rest of the world. Over millennia, humans had forgotten that they existed and soon they were nothing more than a whisper of an ancient religion. While the rest of the world grew, advanced, and developed, the people inside the city had to stay hidden because human fear was a terrifying thing.

Ashar, like the rest of the students, knew there were ways to leave the city. The barrier mainly served as camouflage to hide them from the humans. The problem was that if they left, within twenty-four hours they would lose their abilities and their memories, effectively becoming human without any idea of who they were. When the queen had taken the throne a year ago, she had announced that soon there would be a way for everyone to leave safely, and maybe the city would take down the invisible barrier and reintroduce itself to the rest of the world. It had caused much fear and excitement that after thousands of years, humanity would know who they were again and Rhapta could re-enter the world.

You are correct, Teacher Dev said. *But when the queen said that, she meant several years in the future, meaning five, ten, twenty, maybe even fifty years from now. The queen and her Advisors and Elders are working hard on a plan to do that, but can anyone remind the class why we have to be careful about how we do this?*

A tall girl in the back raised her hand and Teacher Dev pointed to her. *Thank you, Teacher. We have to be careful because humans do not have abilities like us.*

Teacher Dev bobbed his head back and forth. *That's part of it. Who else can take a guess?*

He called on another boy who looked like he was half-asleep. *Um...because that would be a surprise?* Several students laughed at that.

Because humans are fragile and we would crush them! a boy shouted, punching a fist into his other hand.

Teacher Dev ran a hand over his face. *No, no, no. Yes, it's true that humans do not heal as fast as us, nor do they learn as quickly, but they are mighty in numbers and have very advanced technology. Who else has an idea?*

The girl in yellow raised her hand again. *We have to be careful because we might scare them,* she said without waiting to be called on. *They would see our abilities as a threat and that could jeopardize our relationship with them.*

Yes! Teacher Dev exclaimed. *And as I've said before, fear keeps people from thinking clearly. The queen wants to make sure that both humanity and Rhaptans are ready for that day. Therefore, it'll be awhile.*

Something inside Ashar wilted. He had hoped that the rumor was true and that they would get to leave to explore the world. He loved learning about human things like trains and restaurants and carnivals. They had spent a week learning about modern cultures in China alone, and Ashar had been sad that he would probably never see it. He wanted to know what it was like to watch a movie or go ice skating or buy food from a store instead of the market. The world seemed like a vast house with endless rooms for him to explore and people to meet but he was locked in a cupboard.

Ashar listened attentively to the lesson though, regardless of the fact he would never get to visit New Zealand or Guam. Part of the way through the class, he heard muffled laughter behind him. He turned and caught a boy and a girl covering their mouths to hide their quiet giggling. The girl glanced to Ashar, saw him looking, and laughed some more. This behavior was not an oddity around him and only made him want to pay attention to the lesson more, so he turned back around.

A few minutes later, when Teacher Dev had his back turned, a folded note dropped onto Ashar's desk. He glanced around and saw the two students were looking at him point-edly. He turned back and opened the note.

I heard Ifran Toma really wants you as his apprentice since he likes to collect junk so much.

Ashar crumpled up the note and shoved it into the pocket of his pants amidst the snickering. The walls of the classroom were starting to become oppressive and Ashar felt closed in. He longed for fresh air and people who had no idea who he was or how inadequate he was. He tried as best as he could to pay attention to the remainder of the class, but his mood only grew darker as the minutes ticked on.

When the bell finally rang, he launched out of his seat and left the room.

Ashar stalked down the hall toward his next class as students filed out of their rooms. He really just wanted to be alone right now though, preferably on a rooftop.

Ash! a voice called and he turned to find Nasrin waving at him from behind a gaggle of students.

He shook his head and said, *Not now, I'll talk to you later.* Her face wrinkled in confusion as he stalked away. Ditching Nasrin only made him feel worse though. She was a good friend and didn't deserve his sour mood. Ashar was wallowing in self-pity when he decided to take a right instead of a left, down an empty hall. He just needed a few moments alone before heading to his next class to pretend he was anywhere else, so he yanked open the door to a supply closet and stepped inside.

It was dark and Ashar closed his eyes and took several deep breaths. He quickly gagged though, because the scent of fish filled his nose. Had someone left their lunch in the supply closet? Ashar opened his eyes and went to crack the door for some light, but noticed there was already a light coming from the back of the closet.

He realized then that the supply closet was much bigger than he had expected; it was almost the size of a bedroom. The light on the other side of the room was in the shape of a rectangle and Ashar shuffled toward it, noticing that the floor was made of wood instead of the usual limestone. When Ashar got close, he realized the light was coming from the other side of a door. Had there always been a secret door in the closet?

He reached out to turn the knob, pulling the door open with a loud creak. He was practically blinded by the light as he stepped out and his feet immediately sunk into soft sand. There was a whooshing sound coming from not too far away and a warm breeze rippled his baggy shirt. He had to blink several times before his eyes adjusted and he could see where he was.

Ashar looked around and realized the whooshing sound had been something massive shifting back and forth; something he had only ever seen pictures or paintings of. All around him was white sand, and barely ten yards away sat the ocean.

He was on a beach.

PART TWO
THE TOWN

THE TOWN

Ashar rubbed at his head, wondering if he had tripped and fallen in the supply closet and somehow managed to knock himself unconscious. When he found no lump on his head, he looked around again. The sunny beach stretched on as far as he could see in either direction, and the ocean wafted in and out to create a sound like wind through tall grass.

Behind him, Ashar found the door he stepped out of was the entrance to a small shack that sat alone on the beach. He looked behind it and the beach curved slowly upwards and eventually ended in a hill dotted with rocks and shrubs. Going back to the front of the shack, he opened the door to go back inside. There was a small row boat on one side, several oars, fishing rods and hooks, and a pile of nets on the other side of the room. He walked the few feet to the back, but only found a solid wall.

There was no door back into the supply closet. Ashar started frantically digging at the wall, looking for a hidden seam or handle but he had already walked around the shack and knew there was nothing behind it. Finally giving up, he groaned and ran back out to the beach.

Where am I? he thought to himself, shielding the sun from his eyes. It looked to be later in the day than he thought it was, but he could not be sure. How had he gotten here? Was he dreaming? There was not a single soul in sight other than a few seagulls that glided over the waves. With no other option, Ashar picked a direction and started walking.

There was very little sand surrounding Rhapta other than the banks of a few small streams in the nearby forest. Ashar had only ever seen pictures of beaches before and was discovering it was rather difficult to walk so he pulled off his sandals and slung them over his shoulder. He kept looking around as if he would wake up suddenly and discover that he dozed off in between classes. Ashar could already imagine Nasrin's scolding comments if she found out he missed any more of his classes after they had spoken.

He walked for nearly thirty minutes before little dots started to come into view. When he got closer, he realized they were people. There were groups of them sitting or lying in the sand. Children screamed and played in the water and adults shouted at them. Ashar's eyes bulged out when he saw what they were wearing—or not wearing.

Rhaptans dressed for the oppressive heat of the African sun, opting for flowing clothes in bright colors and patterns. Many men would forgo shirts, or some opting to only wear a simple cloth draped over their shoulder.

Ashar preferred loose clothing so he was able to move around. These people, however, looked like clothing had wronged them and they were shunning fabric for the foreseeable future.

Ashar quickly averted his eyes out of respect and made his way further up the beach toward the hill. As he was passing by a small family, he caught a snippet of their conversation. What struck him was not what they were saying, but what language they were speaking.

All Rhaptan children had extensive language classes, even though they only ever spoke Rhaptan. It was part of their studies into human cultures since humans spoke so many different dialects. Ashar didn't necessarily do well in those classes, but he was able to discern what language the family was speaking.

It was Portuguese. And they were speaking it out loud, not telepathically. Had he somehow ended up in Portugal? What was going on?

A few people gave his clothing strange looks but Ashar only hurried up the hill. As he got closer to the top, he could hear a cacophony of noise and when he got to the crest of the hill, his jaw dropped.

Before him sat what he could only assume was a small parking lot. Each of the spaces was filled with one of the large mechanical cars he had studied in his classes. On the other side of the lot, he could see a street that led into a small town which was where most of the noise was coming from. Ashar walked through the parking lot, careful not to touch the shiny cars.

One of them finally drove into the lot and his heart beat wildly at how fast it was going. The windows were rolled down and music was blaring out. Ashar watched as two people climbed out, but no band. He knew humanity had vast and advanced technology, especially in regards to sound, yet it was a marvel to experience first-hand. They could carry a band with them wherever they went!

Ashar could not stop smiling as he walked toward the street. More cars flew back and forth, and across the street he recognized a restaurant. People sat at tables outside, many of them speaking animatedly out loud. That must have been the noise he had heard. In fact, more people walked back and forth along the street, all of them talking out loud. The sound was so unnatural to Ashar's ears, and the silence in his head was so loud without the telepathic speech that surrounded him most hours of the day.

When there weren't any cars hurtling by, he ran across the street and kept following it past the restaurant. From what he could see, this was not one of the huge cities with towers that reach up into the sky. All of the buildings were low, lower than some even in Rhapta, and the streets were not very wide. They all had red or orange tiled roofs and the roads were made of small interconnecting stones.

Ashar followed the street, keeping to the sides so as not to get hit by any of the cars. There weren't as many as he moved toward the center of the town toward something that looked like a smaller version of the central plaza in Rhapta. Hundreds of people walked around a square with several intersecting streets. Ashar craned his neck in every direction, looking at the clothes, the hairstyles, the technology that humans had gripped in their hands as they walked, all while listening to their conversations. He only understood a few words here and there but his ears quickly felt overstimulated, not used to so much noise.

Along the edges of the square were booths in some mock version of the markets in Rhapta. These were much smaller, but people walked between them, buying items with paper. Rhaptans used silver shillings, but he knew most human cultures also used a form of paper or plastic money that he didn't fully understand.

Many of the items being sold were foods he recognized. There were fruits and vegetables and breads, but there were also items he didn't even know how to describe. He wandered around the square, admiring both the people and the booths. He didn't stand out so much here as he did at the beach, and people rarely paid any attention to him.

After walking around for nearly an hour, Ashar sat down on one of the benches at the edge of the square. It had finally sunk into him that he was no longer in Rhapta and was truly out in human society. In Portugal! Looking up at the sun arcing in the sky, a feeling of dread washed over him. How long had he been here? He only had a day before he would lose his abilities and forget who he was. He started to panic thinking of his uncle coming home and not finding Ashar there. Uncle Adil would not worry at first, but when Ashar didn't come home the next day or the next, Adil would run through the city trying to find him.

Ashar looked around, sweat beading at his temples as he tried to think of a way back home. He knew where the city was located in Tanzania, but Portugal was on another continent. He had no money and no identification documents either. It was not lost on him that he was just as poor in a human city as he was in Rhapta.

"Você está sozinho?" Ashar turned to find a middle-aged woman talking to him. She had a motherly concern on her face and a bag full of food at her shoulder.

Ashar had the sudden horror of imagining himself captured by humans and never being able to return home. Or worse, if he gave away the location of the city. Of course, it would be him, Ashar Kouri, who would bring about the end of his people.

"Não falo Português!" Ashar choked out and ran in the first direction he saw. He didn't know if they were after him, but he ran as hard as he could down the nearest street.

His deft feet avoided people, and now cars as he left the square behind. He ran down an alley only to find that there was a metal fence blocking the other end. His heart pounded in his chest and he had to backtrack to the street and find a different way. It took him ten minutes but he finally managed to get to an area where no one could see him as he climbed a short wall and pulled himself up onto the roof of a building that sat adjacent to a church.

Ashar lay flat as he gasped for air. He waited a few minutes before looking over the edge. When he didn't see anyone chasing him, he laid back down and thought about what happened in the square.

All right, I may have overreacted, he thought to himself, replaying the words the woman had said. She was probably just concerned for him. To be fair, his feet were scuffed up from all the walking and running, and his clothes looked a little rattier than what the humans were wearing. He healed much faster than a human though, and any scrapes on his feet would have disappeared already. Maybe she thought he was homeless, but she definitely didn't look like she was going to capture him.

The dazzling awe that he felt when he first arrived in the little town was starting to wear off. It was starting to look like he would not be able to get home anytime soon, if ever. Nasrin would be angry at first, thinking that he was skipping school, but eventually she would worry just like his uncle. Maybe it was for the best though...

Ashar got to thinking that the only downside to this was that he would not remember who he was after a day. It's not like he had any abilities to lose and he didn't have much of a future back in Rhapta.

Outside of the city, he could travel the world, stealing only when he needed to. It would be no different from being in Rhapta, except he would be able to see everything! The only problem is that he would forget who he was, but what if he wrote a note to himself? He could tell his future self everything about Rhapta and its people and who he was, so he could basically be himself again.

That's it! Ashar thought. Now that he had a plan and had regained his energy, he climbed back down the side of the building to the street. He just needed to find a piece of paper and a quill.

Looking around, he realized he didn't know where he was now. He hadn't paid any attention when he was running away from his imagined pursuers. He sighed and loped off in a random direction, hoping it was a good one. It was much quieter in this area of the town, but people still walked along arm in arm. He tried to read the signs by the doors, but his Portuguese was not very good and he could only guess what was inside by peering in windows and open doors.

In all of his studies, Teacher Dev or any of the other teachers had never explained how loud humans were with all of the talking and yelling and music. When Ashar had lived in the outskirts of the city, it was relatively common for people to speak out loud. Many of the people living there would be weaker and some had lost their ability to speak telepathically altogether. Ashar had never lost his ability, nor had his uncle, but he had spent his fair share of time speaking out loud. It was nothing compared to this though. There was just so much *noise.*

Two young girls about Ashar's age came walking down the street, giggling to each other as he passed by. He turned around to sneak a glance and found they had too, sending them into a fit of giggles that had Ashar's cheeks hurting from his grin. It was too bad he could not talk to them, they would probably know where he could find some paper.

Ashar walked along some more, trying to enjoy his experience while searching for the right shop. When he finally found one, he went to lean against a building across the street to scope out the area. After watching the store for a few minutes, Ashar had developed a frown on his face. The shop was exceedingly busy and it was very small; only a few people could fit inside at a time. It was not like one of the supermarkets he had seen images of in his Human Studies class.

He had no money, so he knew that "borrowing" what he needed was the only option and he would not be able to do that with so many people watching. He made a mental note to learn how human money worked because he could have easily picked a few pockets, but he would have no idea how to ask or pay for what he wanted once he had the supposed money.

He waited another half an hour before giving up and going to find another shop. It was only getting busier as the day wore on and Ashar was starting to get hungry as well. He tried to keep his eyes peeled for any distracted shop keepers or unattended groceries, but there was never a good opening. There was a stream of people going down the street to his right so he decided to go that way. He was pleased when he finally came out on the other side of the square he was in earlier.

There were twice as many people here now as before and Ashar temporarily forgot his hunt for a piece of paper. There were a few new booths that had been set up and he inspected their wares. He stopped by one selling crates of oranges and grapefruit; they were huge compared to the ones he had in Rhapta.

A boy who looked only a little younger than Ashar stepped up to the man tending to the cart and paid for a bag full of the oranges. When he was done, he ran back to a man standing a little ways away. The man smiled and said something to the boy, wrapping an arm around his shoulder and an ache pierced Ashar's heart.

He could not just abandon his uncle.

Ashar plopped down on another bench not too far away, wilting at the thought of leaving the man who had raised him. Ashar's parents had died when he was young. Neither of them had any abilities and had lived their lives in poverty, both passing away within a week of one another. Uncle Adil had taken it upon himself to raise Ashar, who was hardly two years old at the time. Ashar had always wanted to know who his parents were as people, but he could not complain when it came to his uncle.

Adil had never been an overly affectionate man, but he tried his best. He always made sure that Ashar ate first and after the bills were paid, any left over money would go toward Ashar's needs. Even when Adil could only buy him the most worn down books or patched over clothing, it was far more than he did for himself. He was only a little over fifty years old, yet looked much older due to the hard life he lived. He got up before the sun every day and would not come home until Ashar was already asleep most days. He spent his entire life trying to do the best for his nephew so Ashar could not just *leave* him.

Ashar groaned in frustration and leaned back against the bench, thinking about the difficult situation he was in. It still baffled him how he ended up here in the first place. It didn't seem possible that he could have entered a supply closet and ended up in another country. Either way, he needed to find a way home, even if that meant he had to walk all the way to Tanzania. He was glad that he at least healed quickly like the rest of his people, because his feet were in for a rough time. This was about to be the longest journey of his life.

A familiar grumbling came from Ashar's stomach. He had just eaten that morning but was starting to get hungry again. His people didn't need to eat as often as humans, but Ashar found himself getting hungrier more often than his peers. Maybe it was because he rarely ate a good meal, or maybe it was all the running around he did. Usually his people only needed to eat one meal every three days, but some ate more frequently for enjoyment.

Abandoning his plan to find a piece of paper, Ashar made his way back to the booth with the oranges. There was a large group of people out front that the seller was tending to, giving Ashar the perfect window to snag a couple fruits from a basket that sat to the side. With the hands of a magician, he slipped two oranges into his pockets and ever so slowly strolled away from the booth. It was easy to meander through the crowd in the square, ducking behind taller people and hurrying to the other side. Once he was far enough away, he pulled out one of the oranges and started peeling it. But that's when the day started to get much worse.

A shrieking whistle sounded behind Ashar followed by a loud, "Pare!"

Ashar froze in his peeling and turned to find two men in matching dark blue uniforms and caps walking quickly in his direction. He started to back up, not sure if they were coming for him, but it looked an awful lot like they were. What would he do if he was caught? He could only imagine what would happen. He had no identification, no parents, and no real idea of where he was. And in less than a day, he would forget who he was too, making the situation even more complicated. What did humans do with children who had no idea who they were or how they got there?

"Polícia! Pare!" they said when he moved away from them and Ashar turned and ran, dropping his half-peeled orange. He was not about to find out what humans would do with him and didn't think they just wanted to chat. Dashing down the nearest street, he looked over his shoulder and saw the two men running after him, shouting. Panic seized his heart and sent his heart into a pounding frenzy.

Now I know I'm not overreacting.

People jumped out of the way as Ashar ran down the narrow streets. He tried not to get hit by any of the cars but did manage to slam face-first into a man riding a bicycle, throwing both the man and Ashar to the ground. As he launched back to his feet, he saw more than felt the long scrape down his shin. Paying it no mind, he was already running again, but the police were catching up.

They must be really bored to chase a child who stole an orange, Ashar thought as he made a hard left across the street, cutting across a car that honked at him as he ran by. He took a sharp right down an alley, jumping a few boxes, and left again out the other side. He paused to see if he had lost the two men, but sure enough, they were halfway down the alley in pursuit.

Okay, I suppose it was two oranges, he thought and started running again. Maybe the humans had a food shortage. It didn't look that way when he was in the square, but who was he to know?

His shin was starting to hurt even though he could feel the faint tingling that indicated it was healing. He was also starting to run out of breath as he passed by a few busy shops wedged side by side. He needed to find a way to put some distance between him and the police and had just the right idea how. There was another very small alley in-between two of the shops up ahead with a large crowd standing out on the sidewalk. There were a few tables and chairs and people were talking and chatting, and some were waiting in line for something. Ashar used his gangly teenage body to worm his way through the small crowd, smiling at the people who gave him annoyed looks as he squeezed by.

In the noise and chaos of the crowd, the policemen's shouting was temporarily drowned out and it was much harder for the two men to push through without hurting anyone. It slowed them down as they shouted for people to move, giving Ashar enough time to run through the small alley, out the other side, and around the corner. There weren't any people on this backstreet thankfully.

He nearly yelped with joy as he saw a ladder attached to the back of one of the buildings and wasted no time scrambling up the rungs to the roof. He hadn't seen the two policemen behind him when he entered the alley, but he also was more focused on escaping.

Trying to calm his breathing, he listened for the two men, too afraid to look over the edge. All he could hear was the noise from the crowd out in front of the building. After waiting a solid three minutes, he dared to crawl toward the edge of the roof and very carefully, look over the edge.

Ashar sighed in relief when he saw the backs of the two men hurrying away down at the opposite end of the street from the alley. He watched as they turned the corner before settling back down on the roof.

Figuring it was a good idea to wait a bit longer, he pulled out the other orange that was still in his pocket and began peeling it. His stomach grumbled in protest the entire time and he thought he would die from bliss after popping the first slice into his mouth and savoring the sweetness. The entire thing was gone in less than a minute and he wished he hadn't dropped the other one.

The street was free of police when Ashar looked over the edge again. He would need to gather supplies if he was going to be trekking across continents, so he made a mental list of what he would need so he could get out of this town as quickly as possible. It was not safe here for him anymore now that the authorities were searching for him.

He sighed when he realized the journey home would take weeks at least, meaning he would still need to find paper and a quill to write himself a note. The sun was past the halfway point and in less than a day, he would forget who he was, regardless of whether he was trying to go home or not. He was not even sure what would happen when he did get back. Would he regain all of his memories, or would he go the rest of his life forgetting everything that happened up until that point?

After climbing back down the ladder, Ashar turned and headed down the street, looking for places where he could steal supplies. As he got to the end of the street, he turned left and collided with two sturdy bodies coming from the opposite way. When he looked up, his stomach nearly bottomed out.

The surprise on the policemen's faces lasted only a moment before Ashar felt hands on his shoulders and wrists. He knew that if they really got ahold of him, he would be done for. Using his youthful body's advantage, he threw himself to the ground, dislodging his wrists from the two men. He kicked and swatted as he scrambled away, the two policemen fumbling to grab hold of him again while shouting in Portuguese.

If Ashar was not in danger of being captured, he would have laughed at the incompetence of the two men. They were nothing compared to the warriors and guards in Rhapta and they didn't even carry spears or swords to indicate their status. Did humans even have warriors? He imagined these two presenting themselves at the warrior's training ring and nearly choked on a laugh. But just at that moment, he managed to get to his feet and was off running again with the laughable humans in pursuit.

Despite his derision of the two men, Ashar knew he really would be in danger soon. He was still hungry and tired from the exertion. Running as hard as he could, he flew down street after street, trying to find a way to escape. Why did he have to investigate the town? Why could not he have just stayed on the beach?

Right now, he desperately wished he were anywhere else; anywhere he didn't need to be running. He mentally chastised himself well enough that even Nasrin might've let him off the hook. On second thought, probably not. She would have told him to stay as far away from the humans as possible.

His feet took him to a quieter part of the town where the streets grew even narrower. There were less signs and it was starting to look like a residential area. The two men were lagging just a little behind, having difficulty keeping up with the spry boy, yet still following him valiantly. Up ahead, Ashar saw a row of low houses with no light coming out from the windows. He took a chance and tried the handle of the nearest door.

It was locked of course. *Come on, I need to get away from them!* Ashar thought in frustration as he kept running and turned down a smaller street filled with homes. He tried handle after handle, but the police only got closer as each subsequent door was found to be locked. Ashar's heart was slamming in his chest with fear as none of the doors were open. He just needed to be able to hide, or dodge them enough to hurry out the back of the house so he could lose them.

In a sudden miracle, the handle of a squat home with an orange-tiled roof gave way and Ashar threw himself inside. There was a good chance that someone was home, but he didn't care. It would only help to distract the police.

Something was wrong with the house though. He was immediately confused when the floor gave way and he was jolted to the side, catching himself on a counter. The floor didn't exactly break, it just *tilted.*

"What...?" Ashar said, in the dark as the floor kept tilting and eventually sent him tumbling the opposite way across the room. The police didn't come through the door behind him and he peered around in the dark. He thought he had seen a window out front that would let in some light, but there was definitely no window here.

He realized the temperature had dropped drastically when he went through the door and had a sudden sinking feeling. He could not see anything other than a few small lights across the room that only gave him the faintest outline of his surroundings. The room was small, with a counter on one side and a little kitchen on the other. Plates, bowls, cups, and silverware were either strapped down or stuck into little slots in a table that was bolted to the floor. There was a single door in the corner of the room. There was also a loud roaring from outside the room.

Ashar pulled himself toward the door slowly as the entire room rocked violently to the other side, nearly turning it fully on its side. Thousands of possibilities ran through his mind, but he could not understand what was going on. Was this some type of earthquake? What was happening to the house? What was making that noise?

He got to the door and pulled it open only to find a short staircase leading up and the roaring was even louder. When he put his foot on the first step, he found there was water running down the stairs. There was a railing on the left side and he gripped it tightly as everything rocked the other way, nearly throwing him back into the room. It took all his strength to pull himself up one step and then the next, water gushing over his feet and soaking the bottom of his pants.

When he finally got to the top, he had to wait until the rocking eased momentarily before shoving the door open. What he saw made his blood run cold.

Ashar stood outside and darkness was everywhere around him. Rain pelted his face and he clung to the railing by the door as the floor tilted again. His feet slipped and sent him to his knees as the floor tilted a little too far and he had to use all of his arm strength to pull himself upright. He was afraid the railing would come loose as it was supporting almost all of his weight. Goosebumps prickled over his skin as chilled air licked at his clothes that were getting wetter by the moment.

A light came into view far ahead as everything tilted again back to its normal position and Ashar could see what was around him. A dark storm swirled above his head, whipping the wind hard enough to send his shirt snapping. He was standing on what looked to be the deck of a fishing trawler. Only, Ashar had never been on a boat before and something felt very wrong. At the prow, he saw two men shouting at each other, each running for ropes or clinging to the rail. They were frantic and wearing much more clothing than Ashar had on.

What Ashar had a hard time comprehending was the water. He had just seen the ocean for the first time today, but this...*this* was something else. It looked like he had fallen through dimensions only to land upon some dark world where the worst of souls were stranded. He peered through the rain and could only make out twisting dark shapes over the side of the boat. Were those really waves? It looked like the boat was sailing through a dark abyss where he would never see land or day again. These weren't the gentle waves he had seen in pictures. These were much worse.

A scream built in his throat as lightning struck, lighting up everything for a single second, followed by the loudest sound he had ever heard. Thunder cracked across the sky, practically reverberating Ashar's bones. It was so close that he was sure the center of the storm was right above him. It stormed in Rhapta, but never had he been *inside* a storm.

The two men had turned to each other and pointed toward where Ashar was clinging to the handrail. He could not hear what they were saying nor the language they were speaking. He could hardly see their faces but he was pretty sure he saw horror on one and confusion on the other as lightning struck again just before the trawler was violently thrown to the side. Ashar was forced to his knees again and his hands were slipping on the rail. He was trying to get his footing again, but kept slipping.

When he finally did, he noticed the light he had seen was a giant flood light attached to the front of the ship. It moved when the ship bobbed, and one of the men had turned it out toward the ocean as the other man made his way toward Ashar. He could not move and only clung to the rail as the ship was carried forward.

When Ashar saw the ocean in the small beam of light, a new wave of terror gripped him so hard he thought he would dent the rail. Ahead of them, he could see the rain shooting across the deck, but behind it were the massive waves moving in the darkness. They looked like the leviathans he had seen in a storybook when he was younger, rising to consume the trawler. The orange he had eaten was threatening to come up as he rode out the lurching of the boat. The one man was moving slowly across the deck, but every time the boat tilted a little too far, the man practically went overboard.

Ashar thought things were starting to level out again when suddenly the nose of the boat started tilting down. It kept going down, down, down and up ahead he could see a monstrous wave coming and the boat was headed right for it. The two fishermen shouted, grabbing onto the sides of the boat as the wave kept coming. It rose up high above them like a god raising a hammer to strike a final blow. Ashar finally let out the scream he had been holding in when he realized he would never see the sun again and would never get to go home. This was the end for him.

In a final, desperate attempt to save himself as the boat was nearly pointed perpendicular to the horizon, Ashar pulled himself back a step across the railing and half crawled toward the door he had come through. His muscles were shaking as he grabbed hold of the handle, slick with rain, and shoved it open before hauling himself through.

Gravity reoriented itself and hard tile slammed into his face as he fell in a sopping wet heap. Ashar lay there for a moment, waiting to die. Yet, the boat had stopped rocking and there was light on the other side of his closed eyelids. The roaring from the storm had stopped as well. He waited several minutes before finally peeling his eyes open to the brightness. His eyes were confused at first, and could not make out the shiny white thing that sat before him while his face was still pressed into the floor. He had to lift himself up before he realized what he was looking at.

A toilet.

All around him were flimsy walls that started several inches from the ground. On shaky legs, Ashar pulled himself to his feet and managed to get out of the stall he was in. To his left were three more stalls and to the right was a door. Opting for the door, he pulled it open in confusion and stopped when he saw what was on the other side.

Ashar had only seen them before in his Human Studies class and it was one of the top five things he had wanted to see in real life.

He was in a diner.

PART THREE
CHERRY PIE

CHERRY PIE

"**O**ut!"

Ashar returned to reality at the sound of the waitress's shoes snapping against the floor, and so did the rest of the customers in the diner. He had seen a picture of one once and recognized the waitress by her apron, notebook, and pen. People who were sitting around the room, slowly went back to eating, silverware clinking as they discreetly watched the woman scold the sopping wet teenager that just came out of the bathroom.

He was still reeling from the storm and his first—and almost last—experience on a boat. He briefly wondered what had become of the men on the vessel, but the smells that were wafting around the room had his nose on alert. It was shocking how quickly his stomach went from wanting to vomit, to wondering if he would be able to sneak a bite from someone's plate.

Aware that he probably looked like he had crawled from his grave, he let the waitress shoo him out of the diner, past the red booths and shiny counter, and toward the door. On the way out, Ashar could not help himself.

There was an elderly couple sitting in the last booth by the door, gaping at him as he dripped water all over the floor. He took the opportunity to snag the plate of pie sitting in front of the man, giving him a smile and a nod of thanks.

"Hey!" the waitress shouted, but Ashar was already out the door, digging his fingers into the flaky, gooey substance. It tasted like nothing else he had ever eaten as he shoved half of the slice into his mouth.

Mmm, cherry, he thought as he savored the treat. There were many delicacies in Rhapta, but he had learned about pie several times in his classes and had never gotten the chance to taste it. He was glad he finally got the opportunity because it was delicious.

The first thing he noticed when he stepped outside was the baking heat that beat down from the sun. The second thing he noticed was that the parking lot was searing the bottom of his feet. Ashar yelped and walked on the balls of his feet to the nearest patch of grass near the street, but even the grass was warm. He realized he must have dropped his shoes somewhere in the little town in Portugal. He would need to steal a new pair before his uncle found out and tried to buy him some more. They definitely didn't have enough money for that.

There was not a cloud in sight as he licked the pie from his fingers, staring up at the sky. There was not a whole lot around him either. He had ended up in a small town again, yet somewhere else on the planet. The people in the diner had spoken English, but that didn't really narrow down the location. All he knew was that it was somewhere hot. And dusty. A breeze carried a small cloud of dust past Ashar, making him cough. Even the breeze was hot.

After licking the plate clean, he set it in the grass, hoping the waitress would find it later. Then Ashar decided it was time to find out where he was. There were not a lot of options in terms of directions, but there were a few more buildings down the road to the right, so he chose that way. Even though there was a sidewalk, he chose to stay in the grass as much as possible. While he would heal just fine, he didn't particularly enjoy the bottom of his feet burning. On the bright side, he would be dry in no time.

Not even part of the way down the street, Ashar found an odd sight sitting a little further off the road. There was a cluster of bright, twisting, colorful objects sitting in the middle of a field of grass. It was surrounded by painful wood chips, but there was a small child climbing all over the objects, his mother supervising from the side. The child was having fun, but Ashar could not tell at first. He saw an awning sitting to the side of the structures with a few benches underneath and went to sit down.

It was marginally better in the shade and he watched the child shriek as he slid down one of the angled structures before climbing back up to do it all over again. Ashar watched this for several minutes before the mother ushered the child to the sidewalk, saying it was time to go. The child whined a little but the mother whispered something in his ear that had the child skipping along happily.

As they passed by him, the little boy waved, and Ashar waved back with an awkward smile on his face. He watched as they stopped by a metal contraption near his bench. The mother pushed down a lever and a stream of water came out, letting the boy drink.

It was a fountain! Ashar suddenly found his throat very dry and waited until the boy and his mother were a ways away before he gulped down mouthful after mouthful. It was unusual that he could be so thirsty after coming very close to drowning to death not long before. He quickly had gone from a climate that was very cold and very wet, to one that was hot, dry, and just as miserable. He settled back onto the bench to let himself think the thoughts he had been keeping at bay since the moment he realized he was no longer in Portugal.

When Ashar had been in his school, he had been thinking about wanting to get away and see human society when he opened the door to the supply closet. That was when he found himself on the beach.

Later, when he had been running from the police, he had been wishing he were anywhere else when he opened the door to the house. He had then found himself on a ship in the middle of a storm. When he opened the door on the ship, he had been mourning the thought that he was going to die and would never see the sun again. And now he was practically melting under its fiery gaze.

Ashar had no doubt in his mind what was going on now.

He had acquired his ability.

Letting out a shout, he jumped up and danced around the bench. He had finally gotten his ability! How was it even possible? He was the first person in his family to have one in generations. It was no small ability either; he could create portals with doors and travel *anywhere.* He was thirteen and thought he would never have anything like this in his life. Was he the oldest person to acquire an ability? He had never heard of anyone getting one so late.

He shuffled his feet back and forth and climbed on the bench to let out a whoop, while throwing his hands into the air. A few people walking nearby turned to look, but he didn't care. It felt surreal. He was in human society right now! It was very possible he was on the other side of the world, and all he had done was take a few steps. He had wanted nothing more than this his whole life and now there were so many possibilities at his fingertips.

Would his life change now? He stopped his victory dance to lay on the bench. He still had to figure out a way back to Rhapta, but he was pretty sure he knew how to do that now; he just needed to find another door. What would his uncle say? He could practically see the man's eyes popping out of his head when Ashar showed him what he could do. And Nasrin! She would be so happy for him and would direct him to the correct apprenticeship immediately.

Ashar sat up, a bad feeling finding its way into his stomach. What would happen when he told people about his ability? What happened when his teachers and peers found out? It seemed like it would be a very important one, so he probably would not have much say what his profession would be. In fact, he would probably be ordered to provide his services to the Rhaptan government.

Looking around, he realized that the sea of possibilities he saw a moment ago was crumbling. If he told the city about his ability, he would not have the freedom to do as he pleased if he was at the government's beck and call. In fact, he would have *less* freedom than he did before, as ironic as that was. He thought about how wonderful it would have been to rub it in Mshai and Jibreel's faces that he had an ability, and one that was a thousand times better than theirs. He could never do that though. He would need to keep this ability a secret if he wanted to keep his freedom.

Ashar crossed his arms in annoyance. *I finally get something good, and I can't even show it off.* He sighed, but realized he would rather have a super cool secret ability, than no ability at all. Above him, the sun looked like it was just reaching the highest point in the sky, reminding him that he had no idea what time it was back home and he no longer knew how much more time he had before he lost his newly acquired ability.

He had to get home fast. This town was small, but there had to be a door in a relatively quiet area. It was probably a bad idea to transport himself across the globe with humans in plain sight. Jumping up, he went back to the sidewalk and down the street, sticking to the grass again for safe measure. There was not much to see but everything seemed so foreign to him, and therefore worthy of awe. The buildings here were rather run down and weren't very flashy or well-kept. People were slower here as well. No one strolled the sidewalks or played outside, most likely due to the heat. Ashar's shirt was quickly drying, but he was sure that it would be stuck to him again with sweat in no time.

Up ahead on the other side of the street, Ashar found a small store with fading display signs in the glass windows. Deciding to give it a shot, he went inside, the small bell over the door dinging. To his left was counter with a rather bored young man sitting behind it. He had piercings through his eyebrow and lip and was staring at one of the little rectangular screens humans carried around.

When the man didn't even bother to look up, Ashar walked around the store to see what type of items this town had. There were many rows of what seemed like...junk. He strolled over to the first aisle and was amazed by how many items were displayed. "Displayed" would not have been the best word because most of the stuff was haphazardly chucked onto the shelves and Ashar saw very little organization in the aisles. Some things he recognized like balls, paper, food, drinks, and clothing. There were other things as well that he discovered were medicine, toys, knick-knacks, and even candy that seemed anything but edible.

Ashar's English was much better than his Portuguese, so

he was able to read most of the labels, even if he didn't always understand what they were for. He meandered through the aisles, letting himself savor the experience while he had the chance. Who knew when he would be able to come here again? He was pretty sure all he had to do was think about the place he wanted to go when he opened a door, but what if it was not that specific? Would he land somewhere in Africa when he thought of home? Would he end up in a different diner anytime he thought of the one in this town?

By one of the windows, he found racks of postcards and flipped through them. Seeing as most of them said "Texas" in some way shape or form, he figured he knew where he was now. On a table next to the postcards, there were at least a hundred figurines the size of his palm.

There were many different kinds but all of them wobbled when he touched them, jumping around like they were attached to a spring. He picked up the one that looked like a cactus and bopped the top, sending the smiling character wobbling again. Ashar glanced over his shoulder at the counter. The young man was still there, not paying attention, so Ashar slipped the little figurine into his pocket.

He spent a little while longer looking through the shelves of items, finding hidden treasures everywhere. He wanted to inspect everything and felt he could have spent a whole week here alone. The freedom he felt wandering through the aisles was unmatched by anything he had experienced in Rhapta. There were so many things for him to discover and he wanted to learn about them all. He knew he needed to get home though.

Ashar went up front and waited for the man to notice him. When he didn't, Ashar cleared his throat a bit louder than necessary.

The man's eyes finally left his screen to fall on Ashar, arching a pierced eyebrow.

"Um, excuse me," Ashar said, heart beating a little faster at using his English for the first time. "Do you have a bathroom?"

The man looked him over from head to toe twice before pointing toward the back of the store. "In the corner." He stared at him a moment longer before turning back to his screen.

"Thank you," Ashar said and went to the back of the store. He took his time, making sure to look over the items on the shelves one more time until he found the door to the bathroom at the back. It was open, so he pulled it shut before taking a deep breath. He was ready to go home. He thought about Rhapta then and the fact that he was supposed to be in school right now. He thought about the classrooms and the supply closet that he was supposedly hiding in.

Taking a final deep breath, he reached for the handle and closed his eyes, and pushed the door open. He was immediately hit squarely between the eyes with something hard and fast.

"Ohh!" he groaned, gripping his face. He opened his eyes only to find darkness so he felt around until he found his attacker. He had stepped on the bottom of a broom and it had snapped forward, so he shoved it to the back of the closet as he rubbed his face.

The closet!

Ashar fumbled around until he found the door and shoved it open, light pouring in to illuminate the small supply closet. He had made it back! Poking his head out, he saw the halls were empty, but he was definitely at school. It was still daytime and by the looks of the sun through a nearby window, it was only afternoon here which meant he still had time to get to his last class of the day.

Glancing down at the dirty clothes he wore and his bare feet, he decided he didn't have time to head home and change. He hoped he didn't get in trouble for the state he was in. Closing the closet door, he headed down the hall toward his classroom. The school was terribly large, as were the several other schools around the city, and he still had to walk a ways to get back to the central hallway.

By the time he got there, he could see it was not as late as he thought it was. Students were still filing into their classrooms, some of them giving him disgusted looks and pinching their noses as he walked by. He didn't blame them; he probably smelled like dead fish sitting in the hot sun.

He finally made it to his classroom as Teacher Farida was just starting the announcements. He slid into his seat as quietly as he could but Teacher Fardia missed nothing and scowled at him.

Ashar, please see me after class, she said before returning to what she had been saying. Several students turned to look at him and some even snickered at his appearance.

Nasrin was sitting up one seat and to the right of Ashar and turned to gape at him. Her amber-brown eyes were piercing as she looked him over. *Is that blood?!* she said to him directly, noticing his pant leg. Ashar had forgotten all about the scrape he had gotten on the boat. At the thought of where he had been today, a wide grin spread across his face.

Don't worry about it, he said to her, and leaned back. Nasrin's eyes narrowed at his change in mood but turned forward to listen to the teacher.

Now, class, Teacher Farida said. *It is time for everyone to pick the mentor they would like to shadow. Remember, this is a very important decision, even if it isn't necessarily the profession you will end up with. I will call on each of you and you will give me your first choice. If more than one person wants a particular mentor, we will work that out after.*

She went around the room, calling on each student who gave their first choice for mentor. More than four students chose a particular warrior mentor, including Mshai. Both Jibreel and Nasrin chose an agriculture mentor, and Ashar actually didn't know who would get it. Jibreel could create small rainstorms that could water crops, but Nasrin could literally make plants grow. Ashar hoped Nasrin got it, and Jibreel would be forced to choose another.

Finally, Teacher Farida came to Ashar. *Ashar Kouri,* she called. *What is your choice? You don't have to pick—*

Ifran Toma, he said quickly.

All eyes in the room suddenly snapped to him. *Ashar, you don't have to pick Ifran if you are not interested—*

I'm interested, Ashar said a little louder. *I want Ifran Toma, the shopkeeper, please.*

It was the truth. While looking through the human store, he had thought how similar it was to the shop Ifran had. The piles of junk he had seen at first hadn't seemed all that interesting, but after exploring the human world, he realized that being Ifran's apprentice would be perfect for him. It was known that the old man was scatterbrained at best and routinely slept on the job. It would give Ashar a chance to slip away and visit the human cities. If he had the apprenticeship, no one would question where he was after school and he could have all the freedom he wanted. If he chose a different mentor, his ability would surely be found out in no time. Besides, he found that he missed the human store already and the closest thing in Rhapta was Ifran's shop.

Students barely hid their laughter, but many of them looked at him like he had grown a third head. His horrendous appearance was only part of their confusion. Just that morning he had wanted anything but to be Ifran's apprentice, but now he asked for it enthusiastically, even smiling as he did so. No wonder the other students were looking at him oddly; they thought he had lost his mind.

All right, Teacher Farida said slowly, writing down his choice before moving on to the next student. Nasrin had chanced a few more glances back toward Ashar, but didn't say anything else. When Teacher Fardia finished, she spoke to the class. *Everyone, remember that I will give you your approved mentors on Monday, that means that those of you who picked a popular mentor will get your final decisions then.*

Ashar could see Nasrin's knee bouncing as her quill tapped on the desk.

After that, your shadowing will start two weeks from now, so be prepared to ask your mentors any and all questions. This is the opportunity to really get to know their profession and find out if your ability is a good fit, Teacher Farida said. *Class is dismissed!*

Before teacher Farida could insist he stay behind, Ashar hurried out of the back of the classroom and out into the hall-way. He would probably be in twice as much trouble on Monday, but he didn't care.

He could hardly hold back his smile as he made his way through the building that had caused him so much stress over the years. Everything was different now. There were hundreds of children around him, yet none of them knew where he had been today. If anyone in the government had found out where he had been, he would be in for a long interrogation. Rhapta and the queen tried very hard to keep the city and its people hidden, so Ashar's escapade across the world would be frowned upon at best. Yet, no one knew.

He had so many possibilities in his life and he was already excited for tomorrow. He only needed to make sure that he was not gone for more than a day, otherwise he could go wherever he wanted whenever he wanted. Cairo, Bangkok, New York, St. Petersburg! There were so many places he wanted to visit and had to resist the temptation to leave as soon as he got home. He had a strenuous day—nearly dying—and knew he needed sleep. He decided he would hold off telling his uncle for the time being. There was no reason to put him in a position where he needed to lie about his nephew's abilities.

Ashar headed out of the school and down the front path to the street, a bounce in his step that was not there that morning.

Ashar! a voice called. He turned to find an exasperated Nasrin running down the path to him. *You walk way too fast. I've been yelling for you since class ended. Don't think I didn't notice you didn't stay behind like Teacher Farida asked you to.*

Sorry, he said, scratching the back of his neck. *I guess I was a little lost in thought.*

Yeah, that's what I wanted to talk to you about, she said, placing a hand on her hip. *What happened to you? You literally promised me that you would not skip any more classes this morning and then I don't see you for the rest of the day? Did you get beat up?*

Seriously? Ashar said, brows lowered. *You really think I got beat up? That's as creative as you can get?*

Nasrin threw her hands up. *Well what was I supposed to think? You just disappeared.*

Yeah, well I'm here now, he said with a shrug. Students were walking by, leaving for the day. *Oh! I almost forgot.* He dug around in his pocket, until he pulled out the little wobbling cactus figurine. *Here, happy birthday, Nasrin,* he said, presenting it to her.

She took it from him gingerly. *What is it?* she asked, skeptically.

It's a, uh...plant that you don't have to grow? he said. He hadn't really thought this part through.

She arched a brow at him. *What has gotten into you?* she asked, bewildered. Ashar had to hand it to her, she was relentless.

Ashar just smiled. *I'll tell you later.*

He reflected on the fact that just that morning, life had looked bleak. Had he no money, no ability, and no birthday present for Nasrin. In a few short hours, he had gotten two out of the three of them. The world was his jungle and there was so much to explore. Maybe he would tell Nasrin what had happened to him one day; it was a far-fetched idea that he could hide it from her forever anyway.

As Ashar walked with her down the path to the street, he watched Nasrin tap the figurine to make it wobble, and his future suddenly looked much brighter.

Author's Note

Dear Beloved Reader,

I really hope you enjoyed a small glimpse into Ashar's life and his struggle to find his place in the hidden magical civilization of Rhapta. What an adventure he had!

If this is your first introduction to Rhapta, you *must* go and read The Hidden Prophecy Trilogy which is the beginning of the story. If you've already read The Hidden Prophecy Trilogy, which is comprised of Cryptic Magic, Erratic Magic, and Infinite Magic then you are in for a treat! You can continue to catch up with Kinza and Zaid in my next stand-alone book which will feature Mikah and Eta as well as Haris and Mitra. Please follow my author profile on Amazon so that you will be aware of my new releases.

In addition, Portal Magic is a glimpse into my new Rhaptaverse series, The Rhaptaverse Chronicles, which will show the new batch of venari as they go out into the human world to save humanity from the ubir. You absolutely don't want to miss it!

Visit my website (LilySkyy.com) and interact with me on social media. There's awesome merch available for each of my series. Also, make sure to sign up for my mailing list to be the first to know about new releases and special happenings such as previews and give-a-ways!

I love getting feedback from my readers, and if you'd like to stay in touch (or discuss my books), join me over at the Lily Skyy Readers' Group. I'd also love to connect with you on Instagram, TikTok, and Twitter! Feel free to reach out to me directly via email at social@lilyskyy.com. You may access all of my social media profiles by visiting: https://smartpa.ge/lilyskyy.

Again, I thank you for reading, and I can't wait to join you on the next adventure!

Sincerely,

Lily Skyy